YA Kilen
Kilen, Josh
The lair of doom /

34028087381944
NW $7.99 ocn905543249
03/25/15

E Li

DOOM

WITHDRAWN

THE GLITCH BATTLE

BOOK 1

JOSH KILEN

This book is not authorized or sponsored by Mojang AB, Notch Development AB or Scholastic Inc., or any other person or entity owning or controlling rights in the Minecraft name, trademark, or copyrights. This is an unofficial Minecraft novel and an original work of fan fiction that is in no way associated with Mojang AB. It has not been sanctioned nor approved by Mojang AB, Notch Development AB or Scholastic Inc., or any other person or entity owning or controlling rights in the Minecraft name, trademark, or copyrights.

Copyright (c) 2014 by Josh Kilen

Cantonfield Kids edition 2014

Minecraft (R) is a registered trademark of Notch Development AB. Minecraft the game is copyright (c) Mojang AB

DEDICATION

To Megan,

For encouraging my silly.

For Sean,

Thank you for being my part-time guinea pig.

More Titles from Josh Kilen

The Tales of Big and Little

Doom of the Three Stones

Shirlee's Revenge

The End of the Worlds

The Lost Princess Series

The Lost Princess in Winter's Grip

The Lost Princess in The Shifting Sands

The Lost Princess in Destiny's Call

The Adventures of Sean Ryanis

Sean Ryanis & The Impossible Chase

Sean Ryanis & The Brink of Oblivion

The Superhero Chronicles

Birth of Moonlight

Non-Fiction Titles

Walking the Narrow Road: Instruction for Christians In Business

Social Joy: Marketing for Artists

Choreawseome!

Go Write Now

Also, Books For Kids Inspired by
MINECRAFT

Rise of the Master Creeper Saga

Golem Battle

Master of the Creepers

The Master's Last Stand

The Glitch Battle Series

The Lair of Doom

The Portal to the Nether

Down With the Glitch

Steve and Dr. Jakesh Series

Mutant Spiders of Destruction

More coming soon!

Steve and the Curator Series

The Terror of Angels

More coming soon!

CHAPTER ONE

STEVE sat at his computer, playing Minecraft and having a great time. It was one of his favorite games, and it was something that he loved to do. The creatures were fun to battle in the game, and he had the ability to do whatever he wanted in the Minecraft universe. He felt like he was kind of the world when he played the game. Steve never stopped until his mother came in and told him that it was time to eat. Sometimes his mom would tell him to do his homework before he played the game, but since he was nine, it only took thirty minutes to finish his homework. That left more time for Minecraft.

Steve loved the game, and he spent every moment that he could playing it. Steve found so many new and interesting treasures while playing the game that he never stopped. That was what he enjoyed, and he knew

Minecraft was the perfect game for him.

There was a secret to it though that made it even better.

Steve was exploring an underground cavern this time when it happened. It happened a couple of times before, but this time it felt different. Steve felt his body start to grow smaller and his computer screen glow. Steve then felt himself sucked into his computer, and after a second he was in the world of Minecraft.

This happened to Steve before, but it usually happened when he was building things. Steve never got sucked into the game at this point, and he wondered how he was able to enter it. Steve looked around when he got there, realizing that he was in the cave he worked in before the game sucked him in.

"How did I get in here?" he asked.

Steve wondered why he was even here. He thought the only way he was able to get in was when he was by his house. It was so cool seeing the structures he created in the game itself, but this time something felt off. Steve could feel the nervousness prickling at his skin, and he wondered just what this was about.

Steve looked around the cavern. It was just like the one he saw before. Steve tried to figure out where to go, but something was calling out to him. Steve could feel the presence of something begging for him to go a certain way. He decided it was time to investigate, and after a moment he started to explore.

Steve moved forward, looking up at the giant lava formation that was nearby. Steve didn't want to get anywhere near that. He didn't know what would happen if he died in the Minecraft universe. He hoped he wouldn't have to worry about that sort of thing.

Still, there was something off about this area. It was as if there was something out there that wanted Steve to go further. Steve could feel the presence around him, and when that happened he knew there was something up. Steve walked forward, and when he did, he heard the sound of a rock come crashing down behind him. This was weird, especially since there had to be someone around to make that structure fall. Something wasn't right.

Steve kept on going though, and when he got to the end of the cavern, he saw a library. Steve wondered how in the world a library ended up here. He grabbed the handle of the door, realizing that it was just a normal door and nothing more. Maybe Steve was just nervous because he had never been in a situation like this. Maybe it was because he was used to only seeing a couple of animals or

the occasional skeleton soldier when he entered the game. This was like a whole new world, and the fact that it was made Steve uneasy.

Steve opened the door, entering the library. He

left the door open, making sure that he was able to get out of there. There were books everywhere, and Steve wanted to check them all out. He didn't want to stop at one book, he wanted to see them all.

There was something off about this place though. He felt the presence that he felt earlier grow even stronger. Maybe it was because Steve was nervous about what would happen next, but he had to take a chance. He had to assume things would go all right. He was just going to take a look around the place and then leave.

Steve saw a couple of interesting books. There was a book on how to craft certain things out of various ores, and there was even a map of where to get some diamond. This place was a treasure trove of amazing things, and Steve wondered just what else he could find. He thought there might be more, but little did he know of the extent of information in this place.

Steve turned a corner and even saw a portal to the

Nether. What in the world was that doing there? That's probably where the presence came from. Steve wondered if it was even a good idea to stay there with that thing around. He wanted to explore some more, but he didn't know if it was a good idea. If he made one wrong step, he could fall into the Nether and then he would have to fight enemies with weapons he didn't have.

As Steve looked right, his desire for weapons was answered. There was a wooden pickaxe, a wooden sword, and a couple of armor pieces. Wow, someone must have taken a while to make this! Steve didn't know if stealing this was the best idea, but what else could he do? He needed the weapons, and it looked like nobody was using them. He would return them once he was done checking out the cavern and making a pathway to the surface.

As Steve tried them on though, he could feel something around him. He didn't know if taking this was a good idea, but what other choice did he have? He didn't know where to get weapons, and there were no materials around to make a crafting table. He was a sitting duck if he didn't make any. That was the reason for taking these things.

As he put on the least piece of armor though, he heard a crash.

"What was that?" Steve asked.

Steve looked around. The place started growing dim, and Steve wondered just what was going on. All of a sudden, he heard the sound of laughter. It grew louder and louder until it echoed through the room.

"Very good Steve. You took the bait. I knew you would. Now it's time to play my game, whether you like it or not. I hope you're able to survive, but you probably won't," the voice said.

Before Steve could find the mysterious voice, the creature moved its feet on the other side of the library's floor. Steve looked around and in front of him were two zombies. They let out a low groan before they lunged at Steve, their intent to kill.

CHAPTER TWO

STEVE was frozen in fear.

What in the world was going on? Why were they coming after him? What was going on? The door slammed shut, leaving Steve trapped in a room with two undead corpses. They groaned as they moved closer. Steve dodged their attacks, but he didn't know just how long he could deal with this.

"I need to get out of here. I just have to," Steve said aloud. He went over to the door, trying to pry it open. It was sealed shut, and it looked as if the door could only be opened with a Redstone. Steve didn't have one of those though.

"I have the Redstone Steve. If you want to get out of here, you'll have to defeat me," the person said. Steve wondered what that voice was. He had no clue. It couldn't be Herobrine, could it? The rumors said that

Herobrine was silent, and this person seemed to love their voice. It was odd, and Steve didn't know what to do.

The only thing that he knew for sure was that he had to fight. That was his final answer and it was the one thing that needed to be done before anything else.

The zombies came closer, and Steve grabbed the sword from his kilt. It felt heavier than he thought, and Steve wondered if he could wield it. He held it up in the air, preparing to strike, but as he did he lost his balance. He fell down, and the two zombies moved towards him even faster. They groaned their raspy groan as they moved closer. Steve was scared, but the only thing he could do was attack. There was nothing else.

Steve raised his shield up when one of the zombies lunged at his throat, trying to gore it and turn him into one. He wasn't going to be zombie food for these guys. Steve kept the shield up as they moved against it, their bodies hitting the shield with a clunk. Steve didn't know how much longer he could hold these guys off. He had to do something. There was a chest nearby with a health potion, which aided him in the battle.

"What's the matter Steve? Don't think you can beat these guys? If you can't beat this, then you're surely not going to beat me," the voice said.

Steve moved up, trying to push the two of them away. From his own body. Steve felt the sweat beat down his forehead. These guys were too much. He had to use his sword or he was going to die.

Steve grabbed the sword once and lifted it up. This was his last chance, and he knew that he had to take it or else. He lifted the sword and screamed. He dropped it against the head of the zombie, slicing it open. Steve did it to the other zombie, causing them to roar in pain. Steve knew they would only be down for a moment. He had to kill them fast.

They started coming towards him once again, but Steve knew what to do. He grabbed the sword and lifted it up again, slicing the two zombies once again. This time they fell down, and Steve noticed they weren't moving. Was this over?

"They're not dead yet Steve. They're not ordinary zombies. They have special powers that help keep them alive," the voice said.

Steve knew he must kill them in order to get rid of them. The first zombie came to and started to rise. Steve readied his sword and then pushed it into the gut of the zombie. He knew it wasn't a lethal blow, but it allowed the zombie to fall to the ground. It was groaning, but then Steve pushed his sword into the head of the zombie and left it there, turning the sword into the head so that it dug deeper. The zombie groaned and tried to get up, but its efforts were worthless. Steve knew this was the only way to kill them, and if he had to, he would do it again. He just needed that redstone so he could get out of there.

Once the first zombie died it was time for the second one. Steve looked around, trying to find the zombie, but before he could move out of the way, the zombie roared to life and swiped at Steve. Steve dodged the attack, his heart thumping at the attack the creature just gave him. He almost died just now, and it was because of a surprise attack like that. After calming down for a second, Steve lunged at the guy once again, preparing his sword for the final blow. This had to end. He needed to fight whatever else he needed to fight and then get out of there.

Steve struck the zombie square in the head, pushing the sword in and causing it to fall to the ground. It was soon dead, and when the zombie let out its final groan Steve was relieved. He hoped that this was the end of it all. He didn't need any more surprise zombie attacks that's for sure.

Little did he know though, that this was only the beginning.

The voice laughed at his actions before speaking.

"Great job Steve, but this was only the first match of the battle arena. You'll have more, and I'll love watching you squirm every time. This next one is a personal favorite of mine, especially since they are cute and cuddly. I hope you can deal with it," the voice said.

Steve saw a new set of weapons show up, all of them stone weapons. Steve knew he had to upgrade, so he grabbed all of them and fitted them on. That was when he heard the sounds of the creatures, but he didn't know where they were.

Steve looked around for the enemy, but before he could find it the creatures jumped on him. They pushed Steve to the ground and started attacking him, the spiders doing away with the few hearts that Steve had.

CHAPTER THREE

IT was a surprise attack, but Steve could handle it. He knew this person was going to play dirty. Steve did lose a couple of hearts in the process of fighting these creatures, but after a moment he was able to push them off. They were jumping spiders, and they loved to corner you before it started mauling you. Steve knew how these things were, and they were a pain to get out of the house. He had to defeat them before it was too late, and Steve knew the trick.

When the spiders came up to him, he brandished his sword and started swiping at them. There were only three spiders in all, but they were double the pain because they didn't want to stay still. Steve would take a swing at one of the spiders and hit them, but then when he tried to defeat the rest they would all scatter. They also loved to move towards higher places that Steve wasn't able to get to. He was trapped down there, waiting for these creatures to come down and get him.

"What are you waiting for Steve? They're ready for you," the voice taunted.

Steve saw a chest with some health potions. He needed it because he could feel his health going down. He grabbed one and started to drink it, his strength coming back to its normal state. There was still the problem of the spiders though.

Steve was annoyed. He wanted to get rid of these guys as soon as possible. He didn't like the idea of having to fight all of these creatures just to get out of there, and he knew that the stakes were high. If he did die, he didn't know just how much this would impact his life. He thought that he might get another chance, but he highly doubted it. He was going to die if he didn't do something fast.

One of the spiders moved behind him, and Steve

could feel the presence of the creature. It scared him to think about it, but he knew that he would have to fight the creature. The creature swooped down, but before it could reach Steve he pushed his sword up and stabbed it in the heart. The spider squealed and tried to get away, but it was stuck on the sword like a spider shish kebab. It was left there for a couple of minutes before it died, and the second it went away Steve sighed with relief.

One down, three to go.

The next spider was a clever one though. It loved to hide and wait until the last minute. It lunged at Steve the first few times, but it just missed him. Steve was lucky many times when it came to that spider, but he knew that its luck was about to run out. When the spider tried to hide in a dark corner and then run out, Steve used his shield to block the attack and then his sword to stab the spider. He penetrated the spider deep but instead of just leaving it on his sword he continued to stab the spider. It tried to lunge at Steve, but Steve had him cornered. After stabbing the spider a couple more times, it finally died.

The third spider was one that used webs and hanging from the ceiling. Steve tried to figure out the best way to defeat that one, but he knew after a moment. He saw a piece of wood on one of the bookshelves and grabbed it. He hurled it towards the spider, causing it to grow irritated. Steve needed to irritate the spider, it was the only way to get it down.

Sure enough, the spider moved all the way down the web that it was on, and at that point it was high enough for Steve to hit. Steve jabbed his sword into the spider, stabbing it three times before it made a dying noise and then disappeared.

There was one more that Steve didn't see at first.

This one was a hiding spider. It was one of the rare spiders that knew how to hide among the area. It was great at blending in, but Steve noticed that it was hanging out on the floor. It was looking at Steve, but he had a plan. Steve moved in a slow manner, waiting a moment before he jumped and swung his sword.

The spider tried to get away, but it was no use. Steve's attack was too fast, and he was able to make a clean blow on the spider. This spider moved away, hiding once again, but this time the hiding place was obvious. Steve stabbed it three more times before it went away, leaving him alone.

"I'm glad that's over," Steve said.

"You may think it's over Steve, but you're far from correct. I have more in the works for you my friend, and I can't wait to show you," the voice said.

There were some iron armor pieces now along with a pickaxe. It seemed like every time he defeated an enemy, he would get something new. Steve took it, upgrading all of his pieces. He even got some more strength from a potion that he found in a chest.

Steve wondered what was next. There were some experience points on the ground from the last spider, and before they went away, Steve grabbed them. Steve looked at the portal to the Nether, but there was nothing coming out of it. Just what did this guy have planned for Steve? It seemed bizarre that he would go to all these lengths just to test Steve. What was he?

Before Steve could respond though, he turned around and saw a herd of ten killer rabbits. They all had their fangs bared and ready to strike.

CHAPTER FOUR

STEVE was nervous. He's never fought these killer rabbits before. He heard about how much of a pain they were in the game, but he didn't know just how bad they could be. He did read a couple of cool books that his friend gave to him about the rabbits, but most of the time the hero had a companion to help him. Steve didn't have anything but the armor on his body and the sword.

The rabbits looked at Steve, their eyes glowing blood red and their fangs ready to tear him apart. They were fast, and Steve wondered what was going to happen to him. He didn't want to become killer rabbit food that's for sure. He started moving out of the way, dodging the rabbits as they ran after him.

Steve noticed as he ran though that these rabbits were fast. Before Steve could get to a point, the rabbit was there, and he could see the rabbit looking at him with a look of blood lust. Steve tried to move away from it, but the rabbits were all around him. At one point, there was a circle of rabbits cornering him. They were all ready to get rid of him, and Steve wondered what this was going to do to him.

Steve gulped. This could be the end of him for all he knew. He knew the stakes were high. He didn't think he was going to survive. This could be bad.

Steve closed his eyes. There had to be a way out of this. He had to think of a way to push through the pile of rabbits and get away from them. Then he could start decimating them one-by-one.

After a moment of thinking, Steve had a plan. He grabbed his sword and lifted it up, spinning around in a circle. He was able to get a couple of them to go away, and Steve was able to move them out of the way for the moment. He grabbed his sword and braced it against his body once again, wondering just what was going to happen next.

One of the bunnies was hurt, and at that moment Steve knew he had to take a chance with this. It was the last thing he could do against these guys.

He swung his word against the first bunny, taking it out. When the bunny disappeared, there was a potion in its wake. It was a potion to help you gain strength, and when Steve found it, he put it in his pocket. He didn't know exactly what was going to come out of this, but he had to take a chance.

The bunnies regrouped and charged at him, but Steve had a plan. He put his shield up, allowing the bunnies to hit that. When they hit the shield, Steve stabbed every single one of them, the bunnies cried out. Some of them tried to get away, but Steve was able to hit them with the sword after that. Each of the bunnies came crashing down, and soon there was a pile of bunnies that were knocked out. Steve knew there wasn't much left in them, but he was nervous about what would come next. Just what did this mysterious creature have planned? And why did he care so much about Steve? The only way to find out was to take out these bunnies and get ready for the next thing.

Steve hit the bunnies, stabbing them all in the stomach. The bunnies cried out one last time before they disappeared. There were a couple of potions left behind, one of them for an impregnable defense and the other one being used for strength. Steve pocketed them and looked up, brandishing his sword and starring in the distance.

The battle was over, and when Steve killed off the last one, he noticed that there was a set of diamond battle pieces now. He grabbed them, brandishing them and getting ready for what was next. Steve knew that this was the last fight, and he had to make it worthwhile.

"Alright, I killed your little pet rabbits. Show yourself!" Steve said.

The creature laughed, but Steve didn't understand. Just what was so funny about this? Steve was trying to get rid of this guy, he wasn't trying to keep him around. All of a sudden, there was a flash of light, and right across from Steve was a person he thought he would never see.

It was Herobrine.

CHAPTER FIVE

THIS had to be a joke.

There was no way.

Herobrine wasn't real. He was supposed to be an urban legend that people used in order to scare other kids into thinking the game was haunted.

But here he was. Herobrine was right across from Steve. The creature looked at Steve with a smile, and Steve felt scared. He didn't want to fight Herobrine, he just wanted to get out of here. What was the reason for Herobrine's appearance? Why did he come now of all times? What was the deal with that?

Steve had a million questions flooding through his head. Herobrine looked at Steve and smiled.

"You're probably wondering why you're here. Heck, you're probably wondering why I'm here. Well, I'm Herobrine. I'm the mysterious force in the Minecraft universe. I'm the reason for so many random things happening in the game. You don't realize them, but others do. Some people ask if others have felt these different things happen to them. Some ask if they notice the trees with no leaves all of a sudden. All of that is my handiwork, and I'm the one who creates and changes the land. I'm Herobrine, Steve, and you're a pest that I must get rid of," Herobrine said.

"W-what do you mean?" Steve asked.

"What I mean is, you're a problem. You know about the Minecraft universe and you can travel here. Most players are not supposed to do that, but a couple have slipped through the cracks. You're one of them. Most of the time though, the ones who slip through the cracks die within the first couple of rounds. I kill them off, and that's what I'm going to do to you. This is the end Steve," the creature said.

There was no way Steve was going to lose without a

fight. Steve grabbed his sword and held it, getting ready to fight Herobrine. He didn't need to fight until Herobrine was gone, he just needed to do it long enough for Herobrine to drop the redstone so he could get out of the door.

"Do you really want to fight me Steve? Do you think that's a great idea?" Herobrine asked in a rhetorical fashion. Steve was getting angrier by the second. He didn't need this creature taunting him.

"Shut up. I need to get rid of you!" Steve replied. He lunged at Herobrine, but before he could, Herobrine sent a bookshelf flying his way. Steve ran into that, hitting the shelf with a thud. Steve fell down, trying to think of how to get out of this. There was a weapon nearby, and Steve grabbed it. It was the Ender Sword.

That was the strongest sword in the game. It was what was going to help him beat Herobrine. There was also a chest containing a powerful potion that allowed

Steve to reach his top strength. Steve drank that along with the rest of the potions, the power making him even stronger. He was ready to defeat Herobrine. This was going to be the end.

They lunged at each other and started fighting. Steve realized that Herobrine was stronger than he imagined. They dealt blows to each other, both of them trying to figure out how to get rid of the

other. Every single sword attack was parried, and Steve knew he had to work fast. When Steve pushed his sword against Herobrine, the creature smiled. Herobrine flew away, ending up behind Steve.

"Don't think you can win that easily," the creature said.

It knocked Steve to the ground. Steve was in pain, but he knew that he had to get up. The creature was on top of him, trying to hit Steve with all his might.

Herobrine hit Steve with a couple of blows, causing Steve to scream out in pain. It hurt like no other, and Steve didn't know what to do. He was trying to get away, but it was no use. He felt like Herobrine's punching bag.

"This is the end!" Herobrine said. He grabbed his sword and pushed it up in the air, his eyes happy with delight. Steve rolled out of the way before Herobrine could strike, the sword being stabbed into the floor.

Steve used this as his chance. He grabbed the sword and charged at Herobrine. Herobrine tried to kick Steve away, but that wasn't what Steve was going for. He moved his sword so that it made a clean rip on the guy's jeans. The redstone fell out of it.

"No!" Herobrine screamed.

Steve knew there was no way he could defeat this guy. He was too strong, and Steve needed a way to get out of there. If he got out, then he could think of a way to defeat Herobrine. Steve grabbed the redstone and lunged for the door. He showed the stone, allowing the door to open before Herobrine could get in. Steve closed the door, holding the redstone in his hand as the lock clicked shut. When Steve looked forward though, he realized the pathway had changed.

There was no rock blocking it. Instead, there was a direct pathway out. Steve could see the light, and when he did, he made a beeline for it. He ran as fast as he could, not even caring what would happen to him. When he hit the flash of red light, he was pulled out of the game.

Steve had his head on his desk, looking around at the place. The Minecraft universe was gone, and the only things related to Minecraft in his room were his posters, the creeper doll that he had, and the game he had on. Steve realized his character was out of the cave and back in his home. He looked around the place, trying to figure out what happened.

Steve fought Herobrine, but he didn't win. There was no way that he could. Steve never fought in his life, and most of the time he hated survival mode. But he survived, and that's what shocked him. Steve was able to live, and that was the most remarkable thing about this.

"I...survived," Steve said.

Steve looked at his computer, turning it off for now. Maybe that was too much Minecraft for one day. He should go read a book or go outside. Still though, there was something funny about it, and there was one thing that Steve continued to think about when he went outside.

He wanted to defeat Herobrine. That was his goal. He was going to beat the creature that sucked him into that game and made him play in such dangerous conditions.

It was on.

DO NOT MISS THE NEXT INSTALLMENT

THE PORTAL TO THE NETHER
THE GLITCH BATTLE
BOOK 2

Want more Minecraft Adventures? Check out...

GOLEM BATTLE
RISE OF THE MASTER
CREEPER SAGA BOOK 1

Chapter One

Steve applied the final touches to his new house, making sure everything was done to his satisfaction. Having worked like a bee on overtime for the past few Minecraft days, it was all finally nearing completion. Steve was excited; his magnificent multi-storey masterpiece was almost ready to be displayed to the world in its full, angular glory. An adventurer without a home is like a dog without a bone, he thought to himself, grinning.

Steve was happy in his work, paying no attention to

the world around him. But little did Steve know that a green-bodied, scowling fiend lay out there, patiently waiting in the shadows for its chance to strike...

Steve finished blocking the last details to his house and looked at it, admiring his work.

"Well, I might not be too hot when it comes to taking out the trash, but there's no way Mom could call me a slacker after this," he said to himself. Steve was more than happy with the job he had done, to achieve things all by yourself was a fine feeling he thought, and made you more confident about doing other things in the future.

As he stood there, congratulating himself on a job well done, a pair of cold black eyes fastened on him, its four small feet propelling it forward in deathly silence; the cucumber-shaped hell-beast headed towards the luckless adventurer.

When Steve finished, he went inside. In a room on

the first floor lay an enchantment table surrounded by bookshelves. Glyphs were being drawn from the books into the table like butterflies to a beautiful flower. He was just about to place a sword onto it to be enchanted when a noise startled him.

Steve jumped, then relaxed. What could possibly be a threat to him in the comfort of his own home? What could possibly ... BOOM!

There was a noise like a meteorite hitting a firework factory, and the building started shaking.

"Whuh?" Steve grunted, shocked. He ran outside to see what could have caused the commotion. A large piece of the front of his house had simply disappeared; in its place lay a smoking crater. This had to be the work of a creeper, he thought to himself, but how could one of the little green beasts have created such devastation?

Steve prepared himself for follow-up attacks, but there were none; it was as quiet as a turkey farm the day after Thanksgiving. Then he heard the door creak open.

"You've messed with the wrong Minecrafter, block boy!" Steve shouted, more confidently than he felt. . He pulled himself together, his health was high, his sword was durable, and his will was strong, time to do some Spring cleaning, he felt angrily.

When the monster appeared, however, it was unlike anything Steve had seen before. This creature looked like a creeper, but there was something darned peculiar about it. Its face was more oblong than most, and it had arched eyebrows over its scowling face. Steve realized that he was looking at a legend straight out of the forums.

It was a Master Creeper.

Steve had read about such beasts in forum posts littered with spelling mistakes, but never imagined one of them would walk straight into his home like a lunkheaded neighbor from hell. It scared him, but he was not going to let this explosive runner-bean shaped intruder ruin his lovely home, no way! The creeper looked like it was going to blow, but didn't. Instead it appeared to be waiting for him.

Steve heard these creepers knew how to regenerate. So drawing the thing out and then defeating it with the normal hit and run tactic was not an option. He had to get out of here.

Suddenly, the creature vanished as quickly as candy on Halloween night. Steve heard a hissing sound from afar, it sounded like laughter.

Steve remembered what the legends said about that creature. It looked like a normal creeper, but one that packed more power than Superman on a punch bag. If this thing could detonate repeatedly, then it was a threat to all the houses in the region, but how can you defeat such a monster? He thought worriedly.

It was no use. For now Steve couldn't figure out a

way. The laughing hiss continued to echo through his mind, and as Steve thought about it, he grew angry. If it hadn't detonated when it first saw him, then it must be waiting for a better time to strike. He could never relax, because he would always know at the back of his mind that the beast would be waiting for him to do so before blowing up like a lactose-intolerant kid after two milkshakes. He was out of his depth, he needed help!

Steve grabbed his travel items. He had a chest full of stuff, but he only carried what he needed - his iron sword and diamond pickaxe, and set off to look for assistance.

As soon as he reached the nearest village, Steve headed for the library, scouring the shelves until, partly hidden behind cobwebs, he found an ancient book entitled Legendary Beasts of the Minecraft World. Like all books in the land it was written in the strange signs that so confused novice Minecrafters. Steve, however, was no novice, and understood enough to know what he was looking for. Suddenly he saw it, the answer striking him like an unexpected custard pie to the face.

Golems! They were the key to it, and not just the standard iron one with a liking for roses, but six different types. It was worth a shot, that's for sure.

Steve put the book back on the shelf and prepared himself for the adventures to come. He was going to find himself some golems, and when he did, he would defeat them and then convince them to help him in his quest. It might not be a surefire plan, but it was the best he had. But before he started out, he needed to use the village's enchantment table; there was something he needed to add to his sword.

Want EVEN MORE Minecraft Adventures? Check out...

THE TERROR OF THE ANGELS

From The Terror of the Angels – Steve and the Curator, Book 1

Steve was snapped out of his day dream by a distinctive scuttling noise. It was like hissing and crackling paper at the same time. He instantly recognized the noise as a spider. Night was falling in the Minecraft sky, which, Steve realized, was still above him. Was he still dreaming? Steve pinched his arm. "Wake up!" He cried, out loud, just in case. Steve was filled with excitement, disbelief, and then, as the noise got louder, sheer terror! Clumsily, Steve reached into his arsenal to get a weapon, but in his panicked frenzy he found himself mining instead. Steve stopped, and blinked, not knowing what to do. He couldn't see his room anymore. Suddenly, all he could see was the flashing of cubes as he fell down the mine shaft. Instinctively, Steve reached to move his mouse, but he couldn't feel it in his hand! He looked down to see where it had gone and found that his arm had turned into a cube.

Steve tried to close his eyes to make things normal again, but he couldn't. He couldn't close his eyes even a little bit. It was like they were glued wide open. Steve tried to understand what was going on but he couldn't. Nothing made sense at all; it was like he was actually IN Minecraft!

"This can't be possible!" Steve's cry trailed behind him like an echo as he plummeted through the empty space.

Steve hit the ground so hard it knocked the wind out of him. His flat back ricocheted off of the bedrock at the bottom of the mine shaft, and his square head smacked right back down on it. Steve was jarred by the pain. Every part of him hurt and he was so stiff he wasn't sure he could move. Out of the corner of his eye, Steve thought he saw a little heart fade away. "Nah, that couldn't be possible, right?" he asked himself.

Gingerly, Steve tried to sit up, but he wasn't moving the same way as normal. It was as though his joints didn't have balls in them. Steve pushed backward with his arms like levers and pumped himself upright. It took all of his efforts just to stand. Taking in his new surroundings, Steve started to believe it was actually possible. Black and grey dappled bedrock lined the floor, and sandy yellow cubes were stacked up as high as he could see. Steve looked down again at his cubed hands and boxy body. He reached up and touched the lines of his square head. He had no fingers to run through his shaggy hair, but that didn't matter because his hair was flat too! Slowly, it dawned on him. This. Was. Real. He was IN Minecraft!

Steve had fallen into a room of some sort, but there was a doorway that must lead to something else. Filled with excitement and curiosity, Steve walked out of the room and down a dark corridor. Cubed torches lined the walls but the light didn't fall the same way that it did in the real world. It only fell in little cubed areas. Everywhere else was pitch black. Steve slowed down as he reached another door. He heard the familiar hissing crackle of a spider behind him again and he knew that it wasn't safe to stay out in the open. If this was real and he had somehow been pulled into the game, then he knew he couldn't afford to be attacked. Steve could see that he only had two hearts remaining. He had been playing in Hard mode, so he wouldn't be re-spawning any time soon. Steve's hearts raced at the thought of no re-spawns. Hard mode meant that his enemies would deal greater damage. This was dangerous! Thinking of nothing but making it safely through the night, Steve pushed open the door and walked inside. The noises grew louder in the darkness – a mob of spiders was gathering! Steve didn't waste any time slamming the door shut behind him.

It was so quiet in the new room that Steve could feel the silence around him like a blanket. He tried to blink his eyes again, forgetting that they couldn't do that. He was blind for a moment as his eyes adjusted to the new lighting. The whole room was flooded with a bluish light that Steve had never seen before. As he swiveled his brick head back and forth, Steve saw that the room was filled with strange statues in all different shapes and sizes. The only thing the statues had in common were large wings on their backs, and for some reason, they were all covering their faces with their hands. They looked like angels. "That's weird." he thought. "I've never seen that before."

As Steve looked about to see if there was another door that he might be able to escape through, he heard something move behind him. Steve turned around, but there was nothing there, just the angel statues. Still looking for a doorway, Steve moved further into the room. There was the noise again, like stone scraping against the bedrock! Steve's spine tingled. Still not seeing another door, Steve began to panic. "There's no way out of here!" he thought. Frantically, he tried to assess his situation and come up with a plan. That's when Steve got the fright of his life: As he stood there thinking that perhaps he could just hide out until morning, a heavy hand landed on his shoulder!

Steve's two remaining hearts raced and he could

hear them thump in his ears. He was so frightened that he froze. Steve put his block hands up over his eyes, covering his face like the angel statues, as though that would hide him. As the hand pulled him backward, he did nothing to fight it. Worried thoughts sprinted through Steve's mind; he didn't know what was going to happen, but he didn't dare look behind him. Steve's health was low. He only had two hearts and whatever had a hold of him could take them away.

"Hello! Didn't mean to scare you there!" came a lilting voice from behind Steve as the hand fell away from his shoulder. Steve turned around to see who the voice with the funny accent belonged to. There before him stood another cuboid version of a person, wearing, of all things, a bow tie! Steve hadn't realized that he had left the game on multiplayer. The avatar seemed to be rolling on his heels as he waited for Steve to respond.

"Uh, who are you?" was all that Steve could muster. Straightening his bow tie with both block hands the other cuboid replied, "I'm....ah....the....Curator!"

"A curator of what?" Steve asked, wondering why anyone would have a job like that in a game like this.

"Ahhh, a curator of things." The Curator replied, emphasizing the last word, as though that was quite obvious.

"I'm Steve." Steve said. He watched in wonder as the curator rushed around a tiny room that was separating them from the statues.

"Did you notice anything strange?" The Curator asked. Steve tried to work out what The Curator was doing, but he didn't seem to actually be doing anything.

"About what?" Steve asked.

Stopping still and locking eyes with Steve, the Curator replied slowly, as though speaking to a small child: "About the angel statues." Steve shrugged his square shoulders. Looking at Steve with confusion, The Curator copied him. "What's this?" He asked, shrugging his shoulders up and down. Steve couldn't help but smile a little as the Curator threw his limbs about.

"I guess it sounded like they were moving?" Steve said with a question to his voice. He didn't want the Curator to think that he was stupid.

The Curator stared at Steve for a minute; he seemed to thinking hard about something, but Steve couldn't tell what.

"You've woken them all up!" The Curator hollered while spinning around in an energetic circle. "You've woken them all up and now they're all... cranky." The Curator finished, wrinkling his nose.

"I've woken what up?" Steve asked, flabbergasted. There was nothing else around but the two of them and the statues.

"It doesn't matter. Just don't blink." the Curator said

as he peered around the corner and out into the room.

Buy the Terror of the Angels Today!

More Titles from Josh Kilen

The Tales of Big and Little

Doom of the Three Stones

Shirlee's Revenge

The End of the Worlds

The Lost Princess Series

The Lost Princess in Winter's Grip

The Lost Princess in The Shifting Sands

The Lost Princess in Destiny's Call

The Adventures of Sean Ryanis

Sean Ryanis & The Impossible Chase

Sean Ryanis & The Brink of Oblivion

The Superhero Chronicles

Birth of Moonlight

Non-Fiction Titles

Walking the Narrow Road: Instruction for Christians In Business

Social Joy: Marketing for Artists

Choreawseome!

Go Write Now

Also, Books For Kids Inspired by
MINECRAFT

Rise of the Master Creeper Saga

Golem Battle

Master of the Creepers

The Master's Last Stand

The Glitch Battle Series

The Lair of Doom

The Portal to the Nether

Down With the Glitch

Steve and Dr. Jakesh Series

Mutant Spiders of Destruction

More coming soon!

Steve and the Curator Series

The Terror of Angels

More coming soon!

For more about Josh Kilen and his books, please check out:

www.joshkilen.com

Harris County Public Library, Houston, TX

CPSIA information can be obtained at www.ICGtesting.com
Printed in the USA
LVOW06s1929140115

422823LV00005B/223/P